Chapter 1

Charlie pulled out a handkerchief, solid white except for the initials CA monogrammed in black in the left-hand corner. It had been a birthday gift from Lucille. He used it to swipe his very sweaty forehead and then stuffed it back in his pocket.

There was no doubt about it. This wagon wasn't going anywhere anytime soon. The axel was broken. They usually had a spare one, but their last one had broken back in April, and they'd never gotten around to replacing the spare. Now they were going to pay dearly for that mistake.

Lucille tapped her nails nervously against the side of the wagon, knowing it was bad news without him saying.

"Near as I can figure we're at least a week away from any folks that can help. At least," Charlie said grimly.

"So we have to leave everything we own behind. Well, we got to do what we got to do. The trails are littered with people who have had to do the same. Michael's going to be hard to take horseback, but I'll try binding him to me like I've seen some of the Indian women do."

"It's worse than that, Lucille. Water's scare through this blasted part of the prairie, and I'm not sure we can take enough water to do us until we get to the creeks the map shows. We'll have to leave our firewood behind, but we can probably get by on buffalo chips. It's the water that concerns me."

"Well, we'll just ride a little faster. That's all."

"We won't be able to ride them too hard. They'll need every bit of the water we do have and if something happens to them, we really will be stranded."

Lucille looked over at the children, Allie who was almost five and nine-month-old Michael. They sat on a quilt playing a game of patty cake in the shade of the wagon completely oblivious to the trouble they were facing. And even if they had known, they had complete confidence in their parents to keep them safe.

Like she and Charlie should have in God. The faith of a child. She prayed to God then and there before they even unhitched the horses. Charlie smiled but joined her in the prayer.

He unloaded everything from the wagon with Lucille's help. They were trying to decide how they could carry the water as it currently set in a large barrel, They could fill the buckets and waterskins and attach those to the saddle, but some of it would be forfeited unless they figured out a better way.

"Maybe it's possible that I can turn the wagon into a two-wheeled cart," he said, "but that's going to waste precious time that we don't have."

"Do what you think's best. I'm behind you whatever you decide."

Charlie should have known to expect miracles by now being a missionary for many years now, but it was still a surprise to him when a wagon rolled into sight.

It was the largest wagon they'd ever seen. There was a door and a roof, and it had four horses pulling it. It was painted a bright red with gold trim, which made it plain they were performers of some sort.

A man in his late fifties or early sixties drove the wagon and halted it when he got to theirs. "You people look in need of some help," he called down from his high perch.

"We are. Is it possible you have room to carry our water and then we can follow you on horseback until we reach a settlement?" Charlie asked.

"I can do you better than that. I've got room for all your things. Your children can even ride inside the wagon. It's me, my wife, and my sister. I know they'd be happy to watch the moppets while you ride your horses."

Charlie heard the but in his voice. "And what would you want in exchange?"

"As I said it's just me, my wife, and my sister. We had to let two of our actors go. If you and your wife would perform with us until we can get replacements, why we'd be indebted to you."

Charlie looked at Lucille. Lucille looked at their things. It would take a long time to replace all their quilts, their benches, their cot, just to name a few things, but most importantly it would ensure their water lasted. Saying yes could literally mean the difference between life and death. The idea of acting didn't thrill her, but unlike a lot of ministers, she didn't count it a sin either. "You've got yourself a deal, brother."

Michael had grown tired of patty cake and was now pushing his sister away when she tried to do it with him.

"You and Michael get to ride in the big red wagon. Won't that be fun?" Lucille asked, interrupting.

"What about our wagon?" Allie asked, looking over at it.

"We'll have to leave it behind and get a new one. Daddy and I will be following you with our horses. Look after Michael and try to keep him entertained if he starts getting fussy."

The prospect of riding the interesting-looking wagon seemed to outweigh her natural shyness and she had no argument about riding without her parents.

Lucille picked up Michael and hugged him. He wasn't the most cuddly baby in the world. He wasn't opposed to hugs per se, but he didn't respond to them either. He wasn't afraid of strangers a bit. In fact, he seemed not to care who was holding him, which hurt Lucille a little, but she couldn't expect him to be just like Allie. And at least she could rest easy that it wouldn't distress him to ride with the strange women.

The man she assumed to be Francis, since Francis' Acting Company was painted in gold along with a rather rudimentary image of him, had gone to inform his family of the arrangements.

The women came out now to greet them.

"I'm Permelia, Francis' sister. I'm so pleased you both will be joining us. I rather think it was fate our meeting, don't you?" asked the older of the women. She was an overweight lady with gray, brittle hair and crooked, yellowing teeth, but her sunny disposition overshadowed any flaws in her appearance. Her accompanying gestures as she spoke were flamboyant as if she were constantly onstage.

"And I'm Evelyn, his wife." She was much younger than Francis. Younger than Lucille and Charlie even. She spoke with a cultured English accent. She was a beauty with a rosy complexion, jade-colored eyes, and blonde hair that contrasted only slightly with her light brown eyebrows. She was born to be a leading lady if ever anyone was.

After Charlie and Lucille introduced themselves and the children to the women and Permelia took charge of the kids, Evelyn and Francis pitched in with moving everything into the wagon. They got everything loaded in no time. There was plenty of space inside. It was more of a house on wheels inside than a storage unit, although they did have plenty of theatre related items in it.

"I never did introduce myself properly. I'm Francis Wilkerson. My guess is you're Brother Charles," he said, having read the name on the canvas before they'd folded it up. "And you my dear lady are?"

"Lucille Addington."

"Addington. Where have I heard that name before? Have you been on stage perhaps?"

"No," Charlie answered right away. He was less than thrilled with this arrangement..

"Well, we do some scenes from Shakespeare and a melodrama that is our signature piece. Melodrama is quite popular right now, especially among these provincial towns, and we have one I'm particularly proud of, having written it myself. Which reminds me how's your musical talent?"

"Charlie plays the guitar very well," Lucille said.

"Good. I can work that in between acts, but what I really need is a piano player. We had to leave ours back in Russellville."

"Didn't you say your mother taught you piano?" Charlie asked Lucille.

"Just a little, and I only got to play when we were at my aunt's house since she was the one with the piano. I'm very rusty. I haven't played in quite some time."

"That's more training than any of us have," Francis said. He went inside the wagon and brought a thick stack of papers. He handed her the sheet music first.

"I can't read this kind of music," Lucille informed him. "I can read shape notes but not these fancy piano notes, but I'll work at it though just don't expect spectacular results."

"You'd be surprised how easy it is to entertain a crowd who sees little entertainment, especially when they're drunk as many of our patrons are. Whatever you can produce will be fine." He gave them the other papers. "We do *Hamlet*, *Othello*, and *Antony and Cleopatra*.

Your parts are underlined. Well, we better get moving. The curtain wait for no man." And he climbed back onto his high mount where he picked up the reins.

A quick glance through the wrinkled sheets as they moved toward their horses showed that there were a lot of lines for them to memorize. They'd been expecting bit parts and though they had those too, they also had the starring roles in *Othello* and Charlie was going to have to be the villain in the melodrama.

"Oh, Lord," Lucille prayed. "What have we gotten ourselves into?"

Chapter 2

"Charmian. Does that sound like a girl's name to you?" Charlie asked Lucille quietly that evening as they were reading the scripts for the first time.

"I don't know. It's not exactly a name you hear everyday. Why?"

"It's the name of my character in *Antony and Cleopatra* and from the way the lines read, it sounds like it might be a woman."

Lucille's lips twitched in an effort not to smile.

"You think this is funny?" he asked, his brows coming together in a frown.

"No, no. Of course I don't. Why don't you just ask him if it's a woman's part."

"Mr. Wilkerson-" Charlie called to him. He was in earshot and from appearances, working on writing a new play.

"Just Francis," Francis interrupted as he came closer.

"Francis, is Charmian a woman's part?" Charlie asked straight out.

"Yes, but don't worry. The last actor who played her was a large man. Not as tall as you, but I think his dress will fit you well enough. Let me-"

Wardrobing hadn't exactly been his concern. "Stop right there. I am not dressing up like a woman."

Francis looked genuinely puzzled by his attitude. "They did it in Shakespeare's day. In fact, my sister dresses as a man for some of the parts. What could be more scandalous than a woman in trousers?"

"A man in a dress, and I don't care one bit what they did in Shakespeare's day. This is now, and I'm not doing it," he said forcefully.

"No one will think you less of a man for it. In fact, I believe the audience quite enjoys it."

"Then you do it. Besides, the Bible say it's an abomination for a man to dress in woman's clothing," Charlie said, looking to Lucille to back him up.

"Well, yeah," Lucille said, "but if it's done in good fun, I don't think that counts. It's the intention behind it, not the act itself. In your case-"

"I'm not wearing a dress."

Your parts are underlined. Well, we better get moving. The curtain wait for no man." And he climbed back onto his high mount where he picked up the reins.

A quick glance through the wrinkled sheets as they moved toward their horses showed that there were a lot of lines for them to memorize. They'd been expecting bit parts and though they had those too, they also had the starring roles in *Othello* and Charlie was going to have to be the villain in the melodrama.

"Oh, Lord," Lucille prayed. "What have we gotten ourselves into?"

Chapter 2

"Charmian. Does that sound like a girl's name to you?" Charlie asked Lucille quietly that evening as they were reading the scripts for the first time.

"I don't know. It's not exactly a name you hear everyday. Why?"

"It's the name of my character in *Antony and Cleopatra* and from the way the lines read, it sounds like it might be a woman."

Lucille's lips twitched in an effort not to smile.

"You think this is funny?" he asked, his brows coming together in a frown.

"No, no. Of course I don't. Why don't you just ask him if it's a woman's part."

"Mr. Wilkerson-" Charlie called to him. He was in earshot and from appearances, working on writing a new play.

"Just Francis," Francis interrupted as he came closer.

"Francis, is Charmian a woman's part?" Charlie asked straight out.

"Yes, but don't worry. The last actor who played her was a large man. Not as tall as you, but I think his dress will fit you well enough. Let me-"

Wardrobing hadn't exactly been his concern. "Stop right there. I am not dressing up like a woman."

Francis looked genuinely puzzled by his attitude. "They did it in Shakespeare's day. In fact, my sister dresses as a man for some of the parts. What could be more scandalous than a woman in trousers?"

"A man in a dress, and I don't care one bit what they did in Shakespeare's day. This is now, and I'm not doing it," he said forcefully.

"No one will think you less of a man for it. In fact, I believe the audience quite enjoys it."

"Then you do it. Besides, the Bible say it's an abomination for a man to dress in woman's clothing," Charlie said, looking to Lucille to back him up.

"Well, yeah," Lucille said, "but if it's done in good fun, I don't think that counts. It's the intention behind it, not the act itself. In your case-"

"I'm not wearing a dress."

Francis could see he wasn't going to budge in the matter. "Well, I guess you could play the part in men's clothing just as well."

Francis went back to his seat, so they could finish reading through their parts.

About fifteen minutes later, Evelyn called to Francis from over at the cooking fire, and he came back, carrying a pot of beans prepared by his young wife. "Time to eat," he said merrily. "Papers away. We'll rehearse after supper and then you two can stay up a while longer to work on memorizing."

It seemed to Lucille that Francis seemed elated for no particular reason unless it was that it had just fully dawned on him he had a five-member acting company again. It certainly wasn't the food as the beans lacked seasoning and were a tad undercooked.

Lucille had fed Michael as soon as they'd stopped, and since he'd missed out on his nap earlier, he was already asleep. Allie, who had been playing around on the piano with Permelia, now settled between her parents on the bench to eat the beans.

"What happened to the actors before us?" Lucille asked out of curiosity after Charlie had asked the blessing.

"Just couldn't afford to keep them on," Francis answered. "They wanted a cut of the cash, and it's all I can do to keep us fed. Food prices have gone up, you know. So when they said pay them or they wouldn't work anymore, I had to leave them in Louisiana."

"You just left them out in the middle of nowhere?
Where are ya'll from originally anyway?" Lucille
wanted to know.

"New York, and it wasn't the middle of nowhere. It
was a town. If there's one thing an actor knows how
to do, it's how to work at odd jobs. They'll make their
way back to New York when they've made the money
if that's what they want. But I've found the South and
its people very charming. Maybe they will too."

Evelyn hung on her husband's every word, Lucille
noticed, as if pure wisdom issued forth from his lips
every time and nodded her agreement whenever he
spoke.

She still thought it was pretty lousy being abandoned
like that, but she supposed the actors knew it was a
possibility when they signed up.

"Did you all get the chance to look over all the lines?"
Francis asked them.

Charlie nodded.

"Just the Shakespeare for me," Lucille said. "I'll have
to work on my piano stuff tomorrow since Michael's
already asleep. You know, Shakespeare is not my
favorite playwright. I don't know why he's so popular."
The Wilkersons stared at her as if she'd committed
sacrilege. "Because he can be off-color sometimes,
but I've no objections to any of the scenes you've
picked out."

"Well, you'll like the melodrama then," Permelia said.
"It gets very preachy by the end, but you got to throw

in the morals for the uptight, religious people. Makes them feel it's okay to come see the show. No offense."

"None taken," Lucille said. "I do enjoy a good morality play if it's done right. Not that we have time to see many plays."

"Yes, well, you'll make the perfect Desdemona with your pure, pious manner," Francis said, "and you, Charlie, with your dark brooding nature, you'll make the perfect Othello. I couldn't have cast the parts better if I'd held auditions with a hundred actors."

"Thanks, I think," Lucille said with a half smile.

Permelia went on about how great the children were after that and supper was soon finished. Charlie and Lucille got Allie to bed and then they joined the other performers outside the wagon, moving as far from it as they could so as to keep the noise down for the sleeping children.

Francis rubbed his hands together. "Time to rehearse. So either of you got any more questions for me about your parts?" Francis asked.

"I do," Charlie said. Francis could tell something was coming from the way Charlie's posture was so straight. "Who's playing the damsel in the melodrama?"

"My wife. Why? Is there a problem?"

"Yes. I have to kiss her."

Francis laughed. "Is that all? I don't mind. I'm not jealous man. It's just playacting, not real life."

"But my lips are real. I'll kiss her on the cheek or turn so that it looks as if we're kissing, but I will not kiss her on the lips. That would be a dishonor to my wife." He looked to see if Lucille supported him in this one.

"I agree this time," Lucille said. "A kiss on the lips between a man and a woman who aren't married could lead to misunderstandings or temptations. A kiss to the cheek would demonstrate affection just as well."

"You two are turning out to be a couple of very finicky actors," Francis grumbled though his mood still seemed unnaturally cheerful. "I hope your acting ability proves worth all this trouble."

Chapter 3

Charlie, Lucille, and the children were ready to go before their traveling companions were. Apparently the Wilkersons weren't used to making early starts to their day.

The door to the wagon finally opened and Permelia informed them, "It'll be awhile before we take off. Francis is in low spirits." From the look on her face and the way she said low spirits, it was a regular occurrence.

Lucille glanced at Charlie, wondering if the man was hungover. He had acted a little strange, but it hadn't seemed to stem from intoxication to her. Charlie would know better about that kind of thing though. He ministered to those in the saloon quite often.

He saw the question in her eyes and shrugged to show he didn't know what it was either. Perhaps it was nothing but an artist's temperament.

They used the time to study the lines while Permelia watched the kids.

By 10:00, Francis was ready. No smiles though and he had a barely audible voice so different from last night.

Fresh water was closer then the map had showed or their estimate of where they were at had been a little off for they came upon fresh water by late afternoon.

Lucille couldn't have been more relieved when she saw the stream. It was no wonder to her then that the Lord called Himself the fountain of living waters. As a girl, she'd taken the value of having fresh water for granted as they'd never had to worry about drinking water, but out here one could never take water for granted and nothing satisfied like water to quench a terrible thirst.

Charlie and Francis loaded the barrels with the fresh water.

The acting company stopped by the early evening. They didn't make good time traveling that was for sure. They all practiced again the scenes and play again. Francis couldn't praise Lucille's acting enough. Her piano playing was another story, but she'd told him not to expect much. He wasn't very thrilled with Charlie's acting, but he muttered that it'd do.

Hamming it up was the preference of the day. Though Lucille's humorous, silly side might not be the first thing a person noticed about her character, she had it in spades, and she was very physical and energetic, which lent itself to making exaggerated movements, funny or otherwise, second nature. It was a strong contrast to Charlie's dry wit and stiff bearing that translated poorly to this kind of acting style.

She probably would have been perfect for the melodrama, but she got an escape because she could semi-play the piano. She also knew how to make her voice loud enough to be heard without yelling. Charlie didn't, and his voice was naturally low anyway, so Francis was constantly telling him to speak up. Poor Charlie looked miserable.

Othello was the one they'd gotten memorized first and the only one they were able to practice without the papers for it.

The scene started with a soliloquy from Othello, and in the middle of his solo speech, it called for him to kiss Lucille.

"This is my kind of job where I'm required to kiss you," he whispered in her ear right before he tenderly kissed her lips.

Lucille resisted the urge to smile, since she was supposed to be asleep.

"O, banish me, my lord, but kill me not!" Lucille begged Charlie as Desdemona a few lines later.

"Down, strumpet!" he said, pushing her down onto the bench that served as a bed.

"Kill me tomorrow: let me live tonight!" She clasped her hands together dramatically.

"Nay, if you strive—" he began.

"But half an hour!"

"Being done, there is no pause," he said, moving closer and picking up the pillow.

"But while I say one prayer!" Lucille pleaded.

"It is too late." Lucille was so convincing, he almost felt a little guilty covering her face with the pillow. Of course, he didn't really hold it firmly against her mouth, but he felt like he was doing a pretty good job of making it look like it, and he was wearing a look of anger. She put up a small struggle beautifully.

Allie's scream pierced the air and then she broke out into a run. Permelia had been watching the children, since she had no role in this one, keeping them entertained with a puppet show, but Allie must have wanted to see what her parents were up to and had snuck away. She'd happened to choose a very inopportune moment.

Charlie hurried after her and so did Lucille. They found her hiding behind the wagon with a tear-streaked face.

"It's okay," Charlie said, his voice making her jump. "We were just playing a game. See? Your mother's alright."

Lucille reassured her daughter by hugging Charlie. "He didn't hurt me. It was just for fun. You see we'll be telling stories to people for a little while and sometimes they might seem a little scary, but they're not real. Your daddy and I love each other."

They both felt bad that they hadn't explained it to her beforehand, but she seemed to be calming down. He squatted down and brought Allie onto his knee. "It's just pretend. No more real than the puppet show you were watching, I promise. You know I'd never hurt your mother, don't you?"

Allie's auburn curls bobbed up and down in the affirmative, but nonetheless, she looked greatly relieved to hear it.

"Or you or your brother either. We haven't got to spend a lot of time together the past couple of days, have we? You know what? We'll call it quits for the night and tell you and your brother a not scary story after you both are ready for bed."

"A princess story, Daddy?" Allie ventured hopefully, a grin on her face.

"I don't see why not," he said, relieved Allie seemed to have put it behind her already. "Maybe Permelia will let us borrow some of her puppets for the story."

"Oh, boy! Oh, boy"! Allie said, bouncing up and down on his knee with excitement.

"That certainly cured her in a hurry," Lucille said with a laugh.

He leaned in and kissed her as they sat together alone on one of the benches behind the wagon.

"We should be running lines. Our first performance is tonight," she said, pulling away after a short embrace, but her smile matched his.

"Well, I think I need more help with our kissing scene. How does it go again?" he asked, leaning in once more.

"Not like this," she said, putting her arms around him and losing herself on his insistent lips.

It seemed they never had a moment alone anymore between all the people and the next moment proved it.

"I'm sorry to interrupt," Evelyn said, looking embarrassed to have to do so. "But Francis found our temporary stage and alerted the community of our performance. We have to get it ready."

"Oh, no need to apologize. We were just rehearsing," she said.

"So that's what they're calling it these days," Charlie teased, not embarrassed in the least. They were married after all and all they'd been doing was kissing. Passionately, true, but still just kissing.

"Oh, hush up," she said with a pretend frown that ended in a smile. "Nobody asked you."

Chapter 4

Their stage was the inside of a dilapidated barn.

"It's not the Globe, but it'll do," Francis said.

They all spent the next hour or so, getting the barn ready: organizing the props, the scenery, bringing the lightweight piano in. Charlie and Lucille loaned them the use of their revival benches for the audience to sit on. Then they worked on getting themselves ready.

"I know a lady like you has never worn makeup before," Evelyn said as she prepared to apply the powder and rouge on Lucille.

"Well, would you believe I have? I can put it on if you're pressed for time."

"Oh, you've acted before?" Evelyn asked with interest as she gave the brush over while she got out the mirror, so that they could see what they were doing.

"Not exactly. A fit of rebellion. I wanted to look like some of the ladies in town. I was too innocent to realize why they were wearing it "

"Oh, oh," Evelyn said, realizing at once the only other profession that called for makeup. "We're not considered fit for polite society either, you know."

"I know, but I think you're fit company as does Jesus."

"Maybe so. Just don't be surprised when the local women snub their noses at you even the one that pay to see you onstage." Lucille applied the last of the red rouge to her lips and Evelyn gave a nod of approval. And they both heard Charlie bellowing from where the men were getting ready.

"I guess that's my cue," Luciclle said ruefully. She went over to the closed off area. "Honey, what's wrong?" she called, not moving the sheet in case Francis wasn't fully dressed.

Charlie almost pulled the sheet off the rope, moving it to tell her. "I wasn't going to wear a dress, and I'm for sure not wearing makeup."

"Will you please explain to your husband that Othello is a dark man and needs dark makeup? The makeup is not going to make him look like a girl."

"He's right," Lucille said. "You can't really tell the men are wearing makeup. You'd probably look funny if you didn't especially with lines like 'nether lip'. Why don't you just try it before you rail against it?"

Charlie looked at Francis. Francis had yielded on the dress. Maybe he could yield on this. He looked back at Lucille. "Okay, but you're putting it on."

So Lucille did under Francis' direction because changing someone's race with makeup was far beyond her limited skill. It took longer than her own had, and the result was less than stellar, but the waning light would hide any imperfections in the makeup application. She removed the towel that had been protecting his costume off his shoulders. "I guess it's about that time, ain't it?"

Francis agreed, and Lucille and Charlie prepared to take their places.

"You look beauty-ful," Allie said to her mother when she ran into her on the way there.

Allie was about to say something to her father and from her scrunched up nose it wasn't going to be as complimentary. Lucille intervened before Charlie changed his mind about performing. "Bedtime."

"I want to see the show," Allie said.

"Not tonight, sweetheart. Another night." Lucille might have made an exception to her bedtime if some of the audience that had began to gather hadn't looked like they'd been in their cups.

"I'm not a baby. I think I should get to stay up later than Michael."

"Oh, you do, do you?" Charlie said. "Well, we'll talk about it tomorrow."

"Okay," Allie said with a sigh, clearly not happy that she hadn't won the right to stay up and see the show.

Charlie and Lucille had just enough time to tuck their children in before the show began.

The lineup went *Othello*, *Anthony and Cleopatra*, *Hamlet*, and ended with the melodrama. Roughly an hour altogether including the musical performances Evelyn and Charlie did in between while the rest of them changed out the scenery and costumes.

The audience was appreciative of the entertainment and applauded them for it even though they'd flubbed a line or two here or there and their acting had been only passable in places, which showed how infrequently diversions like Francis' came through.

"That didn't go so bad," Charlie said to Lucille afterwards though he was relieved it was over.

"Not at all," she agreed, "considering it was our theatrical debut. Did you notice I only hit three wrong notes on the piano?"

"You couldn't tell it."

Despite their comments, they were both more than ready for a big city where Francis could scare up some real actors. They wanted to get back to their ministry. They weren't far from Austin, Texas now. He should find two willing people there easy enough.

Chapter 5

The bright red wagon rode into the capital of the young country of Texas not many days later. Austin's population was near a thousand. They could play here at least a couple of nights. Maybe more.

It didn't look like a city though. Pigs were running loose in the streets. Congress Avenue was just a muddy street dotted with cabins and shanties. There was one particularly large and elegant building, but one of the locals informed them it was not the capitol but the French Legation.

There was certainly no theater yet, so Francis decided to perform it outdoors, which was better anyway since they used live horses in the melodrama.

Charlie and Lucille looked out to see the size of the audience this time. It was larger than their last audience. About fifty people all told. They couldn't but notice the first two rows were all filled with young, bearded men. Their ages ran from teens to mid twenties.

"Look at all those men. Is it the fashion to wear beards like that in Texas?" Lucille wondered aloud.

"They're fake. Look. A lot of them don't match their hair color at all."

"Well, why in the world would they wear phony beards to see a play?"

"My guess is their mommas or their wives wouldn't approve or maybe just the local priest or preacher, so that's their sad attempt to disguise themselves. I don't know who they think they're fooling in those things. Austin may be big, but it's not that big that folks are going to think a bunch of mysterious bearded strangers came in to see the play. One or two might've gotten away with it."

Lucille tsked and shook her head disapprovingly.

"We better get into our positions," Charlie said.

She laid down on the makeshift bed, still wearing a frown.

"You're not supposed to frown until I start to kill you," Charlie joked in a whisper.

That caused a smile to form.

They cast a look over at Allie, who sat Indian style in the rough buffalo grass and who they had allowed to watch from the side as long as she stayed quiet. They waved at her and she waved back before the performance began, which went a lot smoother than the last one.

Charlie noticed Lucille kept eyeing the men when it wasn't her turn to speak though. And her frown was back full force an hour later. "I'm going to give those boys a talking to about honesty."

He knew there'd be no talking her out of it. He went with her in case some of the "boys" weren't so polite.

"You fellows ought to be ashamed of yourselves," she said. "If you can't do something without being deceitful in your appearance, chances are you shouldn't be doing it. That's lying the same as if ya'll was doing it with your tongues. Whoever you all are hiding from, you should've just told them you was coming cause you didn't think it was wrong. You all have made it wrong whether it is or it ain't. And ya'll should be doubly ashamed if it's a parent you're hiding from cause that's not obeying them."

They looked confused as if they couldn't quite believe the meek Desdemona was now giving them a tongue lashing over coming to see a play that must've been her bread and butter.

"Ya'll understand what I'm saying? God expects better from us. You all need to be honest in all your dealings. 'By your fruits are ye known' and I'm sure everyone of you's going to be in church tomorrow. Right?"

"Yes, ma'am," most of the boys mumbled.

"Good. I hope to see all of ya'll there then with your real faces on," she continued.

Francis had been watching this transpire with folded arms and as soon as the men had all filed out, false beards and all, he came over. "It doesn't make good business sense to lecture your audience," he said to Lucille.

"It does in *my* business," she said, a reminder to him that they were only temporary. "I had to set them straight. You planning on holding auditions tomorrow or Monday rather, being that tomorrow's the Sabbath?"

"Oh, of course, I do. Am. Of course, I am."

***

Sunday dawned, and Charlie and Lucille got themselves and their children into their Sunday best. Permelia was outside the wagon, blocking the door to the wagon.

"Is Francis not feeling well again?" Lucille asked with some concern, her Bible cradled in one hand and her son in the other.

"No, nor Evelyn either. I have to stay and take care of them of course."

"Maybe I should check on them. I learned a number of remedies from my grandmother." She handed Michael off to Charlie.

"That's nice, but it's nothing a little time and rest won't fix. Don't let us keep you from going to church."

Both Lucille and Charlie looked at each other. They got the distinct feeling that more was going on here than met the eye, but they went onto church as per Permelia's request.

Worship was held in a log house.

The pastor introduced himself. "I'm Reverend Josiah Whipple. Recently of Illinois. You must be some of the actors everyone is talking about."

"In a manner of speaking," Charlie explained. "It's not our normal profession. We're returning a favor. They rescued us when we were stuck out in the wilderness."

"Ah," he seemed to warm to them considerably on hearing that though not as much as he might have. "It's the devil's work acting is. It can make good things seem bad and bad things seem good."

"I suppose that depends on what it is you're acting, don't it? It can be God's work too," Lucille argued, "especially if it's a biblical story you're performing and making alive for the people."

He seemed less sure of his position at her words but then regained his confidence. "Mark my words, actors will be the downfall of our nation's morals some day as the prostitutes are the downfall of the family."

Maybe there was a grain of truth in there somewhere, but she hoped he preached straight from the Word during his sermon and didn't stray into his personal pet peeves for she believed there was nothing inherently wrong with acting.

The service started almost as soon as they sat down. Reverend Whipple went up to the front of the church accompanied by not only a rifle but a pistol too. And the Bible, of course.

"That's an interesting choice, being armed at the pulpit," Lucille whispered.

"Hopefully, it's not a sign of his poor preaching," Charlie joked. "It's probably in case of an Indian raid or a Mexican invasion, which is smart. I don't like that I have to, but you know I wear my gun to church too. I'm sure he feels the same."

"I know. A necessary evil in these times, I reckon."

The sermon did stick to scripture or they would've left, but they were met with many unwelcome gazes.

Chapter 6

Francis was up when Addingtons returned.

"Is your wife any better?" Lucille asked.

"Evelyn's still not feeling well," he said, his voice not betraying anything one way or the other.

"That's what I heard, but you seem to have recovered," she said, the question in her tone.

"I just have a hard time getting going some mornings."

"I see. Well, I find prayer helps me get going."

"I'll keep that in mind," he said with a smile, but it was plain he was wasn't really going to pray.

"Let me see if there's anything I can do," Lucille said, lifting her skirt to climb into the wagon.

Francis blocked her with a hand to the shoulder, which she quickly pulled away from.

"She'd rather not be disturbed. Perhaps tomorrow, but being that Evelyn won't be up to performing, I need your help. My sister's going to take the parts of Cleopatra and Ophelia, but I need you to be Clara."

"Can't your sister do that part too?"

"My sister's nowhere near to looking like an innocent, young woman like the part calls for. You'll do great. I have confidence in you."

He was nowhere near looking like a young hero, but that didn't stop him. She really didn't feel like learning a major part in a short amount of time. "What about the piano? Nobody else can play."

"We did without it when we lost our first piano player. We can do without it again until Evelyn recovers."

So she spent the rest of the afternoon memorizing yet more lines while Charlie got to enjoy playing with the kids.

A lot later, Permelia helped find her a costume for the part and a wig, so she would look different from Desdemona.

"Don't say a word. Not a single word," Lucille said to Charlie as she came out in a silly-looking blue dress and hat but most noticeably she now sported two blonde pigtails.

He came closer to her. "They wouldn't let you keep that wig, would they? Cause to tell you the truth, I'm kind of liking you as a blonde." He reached out and touched her fake hair as if it enticed him.

"You're cute. Real cute," she said without amusement.

"Why thank you," he said, drawing her against him "You're not so bad yourself."

He kissed the tip of her nose. Then he bent down further to kiss the corner of her lips. She was smiling now that he'd teased her into a better humor, and she lifted her face up and turned her head, signaling she was ready for a real kiss, and he was about to give her one when Francis interrupted.

"We need a dress rehearsal since we haven't had one with Lucille," he informed them.

Charlie sighed. The only kisses he was getting from Lucille these days were staged ones. The man never rested except when he was sick. He wanted to rehearse or ride all day and perform all night. He was going to help the man hold auditions tomorrow.

"You'll just exchange the hat for a veil during the wedding scene," Francis said. "Did you get the veil?"

"No, but I will," she answered.

"You do know my wife's off limits, don't you?" Charlie warned. "You're going to have to stage your kiss with her."

"I figured as much, but now you don't have to stage a kiss for your kissing scene with her."

While Evelyn was clearly the better Shakespearean actor, Charlie thought Lucille did better at this melodrama stuff than any of them like he'd thought she would.

In the play, Charlie was an "Irish" landlord, nameless but secondary only to the hero in lines, and Clara was a recently orphaned maiden who had no way to pay the rent. The landlord tries to get Clara to marry him, but she stubbornly refuses being in love with the miller's son, also nameless as Clara only calls him things like "beloved" and "my hero" with the landlord having his own choice terms for him.

It escalates until the villain kidnaps her to try and force her virtue, and the hero has to save the day. In the end, the miller's son and Clara get married and decide to set sail to America, the land of opportunity.

The lines were as corny as the gestures and the music that normally underscored the emotions, but the special effects were impressive. The horses Charlie and Francis rode were trained to leap and charge, and Francis was amazingly still limber enough to jump off his horse and rescue Clara. But even more impressive was the fire. It made a circle around Clara while they battled over her, producing real heat but confined to its circle and was put out by a charming "snowfall".

The Clara-and-the-landlord kiss came, and Charlie planted a sloppy, wet kiss on her. It initiated the proper surprise and disgust without the need to act, which had no doubt been his intention.

"You'll pay for that later," she whispered before he had finished tying her to her pole.

"I hope so," he teased back.

She did what all the damsels in distress did and warned the villain she was going to be rescued by the hero. "My beloved will come for me."

"The miller's son?" He laughed dryly. "No, the parson's already been sent for, my dear. You'll be married to me before the day is through and wife to me before the sun rises again."

But of course, good triumphed over evil once again. A contrived ending as one wondered where the miller's son learned to swordfight and leap off horses, but it was a romantic one and who could argue with a happy ending? Lucille wished life produced such happy, fairy tale endings.

But this life was never meant to have a happy ending. It was the next life that did. And maybe that's why the audience really had no complaint with the cheesy story. It gave them a taste and a longing for things to come and an entertaining break from the hardness of this one.

Chapter 7

Evelyn was up the next day and wearing makeup when it wasn't time to perform. That seemed to say it all, especially as it was heavy around the eyes. She walked right on by without saying a word to Lucille or Charlie.

"I don't care if it's his wife or not. Normally, I don't like prying into people's private affairs, but any man who would hit a defenseless woman deserves a beating," Charlie said angrily. "That's just not of the Lord."

"It's not, but I'll see if I can't talk to her. Get her to open up. Maybe we're jumping to conclusions and she's only hiding circles from sleeplessness."

"That could be, I guess," Charlie said, calming down a little.

Lucille didn't get her chance to talk with Evelyn because Francis came bursting into their camp with news. "We've been invited to perform at a dinner party by the Comte de Saligny himself," he said with obvious pride.

"The man that lives in the fancy French place?" Lucille asked.

"The very one," Francis answered, still beaming.

"Did you find actors to replace us?" Charlie asked. That had been his reason for being out, not this.

"Not yet, but I'm working on it," Francis promised. "This will be a feather in our cap. People will be lining up wanting to work with us after this."

They got only what could be carried in their hands and went to the frame house on the hill for the dinner party and they were relegated into the basement by a servant.

"What's this?" Lucille asked as Allie clung to her in the near pitch blackness and Michael started to cry.

The servant lit candles. "The dinner's not quite over. The comte wishes you to wait here until he's ready for you."

"In the basement? This big spacious house and this is the only place he could find room for us?"

"Oui, madame. He will send me for you just as soon as he's ready for the performance." Then he left them there with just three burning candles.

The acting troupe hadn't batted an eyelash through it all. They were apparently used to this sort of treatment. It wasn't that Lucille had been expecting to sit down and eat with them, but they hadn't even been afforded the courtesy of waiting with the servants. A clear message that they were seen as less than even the servants.

"It never fails to amaze me how folks treat other human beings as if the Lord didn't make us equal in His sight," Charlie said grouchily.

"Don't be scared," Lucille said to Allie. "It's kind of fun down here with the candles, aint't it?"

Allie nodded though she didn't look convinced as she eyed a cobweb in the corner closest to them.

Lucille noticed a wheezing sound. At first, she feared it was Charlie, but it was Francis that was having the breathing trouble.

"Do you have asthma?" she asked.

He shook his head.

"Consumption?

Again he shook his head.

"Well, I guess this damp air ain't helping nobody," Lucille said. She looked at Evelyn and Permelia who seemed unconcerned by Francis' episode.

I've half a mind to leave," Charlie grumbled, having just gotten Michael to stop crying by bouncing him constantly on his knee. "I know you're being paid, but whatever the amount is, it isn't enough to put up with this."

"I beg to differ," Francis said, finding enough breath to talk. He was slowly recovering his air except for the occasional wheeze.

They waited in the dank darkness for about twenty minutes before the servant came to get them.

"One of the maids will watch the children," he informed them. He looked at Allie and Michael as if they were a great inconvenience. Were actors not allowed to have children?

"That would be fine," Lucille said, "as long as they're nearby where I can hear them."

He hadn't been asking her permission, but he nodded anyway.

"The count has a fine home here," Lucille said.

"For the location, yes, but it's his last day here," the servant said.

"Oh, really. Returning home to France?" Lucille asked.

"Just New Orleans. I'm sure you've heard of the War of Pigs. I believe it has become much well-known. One for the history books, no?"

"We haven't heard. You're having a war over pigs?" Lucille asked, not sure she'd heard right.

"Oh, that's nothing. There was a war over chickens about a hundred years ago. Perhaps the French weren't cut out to farm in Texas. Anyway, I shall be glad to get back to a French community."

Lucille didn't know whether the servant was pulling her leg or not, but they were outside the drawing room, so there was no time to further learn about this mysterious war.

The Comte and his guests were sitting around and smoking after dinner cigars and drinking brandy.

They put on the production though the men were rude enough to talk through parts of it.

"Well, we hope you enjoy New Orleans," Lucille said when it was over. No doubt she was breaking some rule by addressing him, but she didn't care. She didn't hold people with titles on a pedestal and she had a feeling neither did the Texans, which was probably why he was leaving.

"Merci. I can't get away from this crude and uncivilized republic fast enough. You won't soon see me around here again. I can promise you that. If you people had any sense, you'd get as far away from Texas as you possibly could too."

Lucille's curiosity was piqued again. "Why?"

"Pigs have been eating my corn and rummaging through my home and no one in this sorry excuse for a capital cares. Even the pigs have more manners than the people here."

"Surely it's not as bad as all that," Lucille said.

"Worse. Those blasted pigs have eaten my imported linens. They even made themselves at home in my bedroom." His anger made his French accent thicker. "They ate my diplomatic reports. Was it not my right to kill any pigs I found trespassing? But no I am to be taken to court to pay Bullock for the lost pigs. I refuse to appear, and I leave in the morning."

Lucille was glad to hear the only casualties in this war were pigs.

"Are you allowed to pack up and leave as a dignitary?" Charlie asked. "Surely the court would have been on your side if you'd appeared. And it couldn't be good for the relations between Texas and France if you just up and leave."

"I'm not so sure it would go in my favor, and who are you to tell me what to do?"

Actors weren't allowed to have an opinion on politics either apparently. "Nobody at all, Count," Charlie replied. "We were put on earth solely for your amusement."

Charlie whispered to Lucille as they left, "I can see why I heard some of the townspeople calling him No-Count."

"He is a man who could use a little more God and little less pride," Lucille agreed.

Chapter 8

Evelyn steered clear of Lucille as if she suspected she wanted to talk with her and went to bed early. And then the Wilkersons had all gone out when they got up the next day. Hopefully, they were holding auditions somewhere.

The Texas heat was being its miserable self today. It wasn't a terrible humid heat, but neither Lucille or Charlie wouldn't have been surprised if it was in the 100s, so they decided to take advantage of the river.

While Charlie and Allie played in the river, Lucille sat with baby Michael on the bank just letting her feet dangle in the water.

Allie eventually came out to play with Michael on the bank, trying to teach him to like the water with playful, little splashes from the bucket. Judging from the mean looks and the fact he kept pulling away from her, it wasn't working.

"Why couldn't the Lord have called us to share the good news in a colder climate?" Lucille asked. "Like Canada."

Charlie chuckled. "Canada does sound real good right about now." Resting his hands on her thighs, he tried to entice her into the water. "You know though you wouldn't be so hot if you were down here with me."

"But I didn't bring a dress for bathing."

He came at her with arms outstretched.

"Stop. You're going to get me wet," she said with a laugh as she planted her hands in his hair to playfully hold him back.

He grinned wickedly. "That's the idea."

"So help me if you-"

He straightened and peered over her shoulder.

"What?" she asked, thinking the kids were into something and turning with him, but his eyes were on an advancing young man.

"Looks like company," Charlie said.

With her bare calves exposed and no shoes, she quickly pulled her feet up out of the water and hid them beneath her skirt.

The man brought with him one of the two posters Francis had put up when they'd first arrived. "I've been looking for you both everywhere," he told them. "I knew you had to be around here somewhere. Can you sign this?" He had brought ink and a pen too.

Charlie dried his hands on Lucille's skirt, so he wouldn't get the poster wet and signed. Then Lucille signed. The man went on and on about the melodrama and how great they were in it. They remained polite, but Charlie finally suggested that he get Francis to sign it too to be free of the talkative fan.

"Why did he want ya'll to put your names on the paper?" Allie asked, having quietly watched the exchange.

"Oh, people do that sometimes," Lucille said. "I guess it helps them remember what a good time they had watching the play. I reckon we better see about getting lunch."

"Oh, good. I'm starving. I haven't eaten in years," Allie exclaimed dramatically.

"I think you've been spending too much time with actors. You had a pretty good breakfast just this morning as I remember it," Charlie, in the middle of putting his dry shirt on, said with a smile.

The Wilkersons were still gone. "That's a good sign, I guess. Must be meeting with some luck," Lucille said. "I'll go ahead and make a big lunch in case they come back. We can always have it for leftovers if they already ate. But first," she said, turning to her daughter, "you need some dry clothes, missy, and your brother needs a dry diaper."

"I'll get them," Charlie offered. He came back with more than just the items sent for, but he waited until Lucille had gotten the children changed to show the extra thing to her.

He held up a clear, corked bottle half-filled with dark liquid inside and a label with the words 'Tincture of Opium' in large letters.

"Laudanum?" she asked. It was a common enough medicine. "Maybe they just keep it for emergencies."

"No, I knew something was off about Francis and so did you. This explains it."

"I guess it does," she said with a sigh, not wanting it to be true, but knowing it was. It explained so many of his daily habits.

***

"Can I speak to you for a moment alone?" Charlie asked Francis that evening.

"Sure. What can I help you with?" he asked when they'd moved off a ways.

He answered by holding up the bottle.

"Why do you have my tincture?" Francis asked.

"Because you seem to be a healthy man. What's ailing you that you think you need to take it regular?"

He saw no reason to deny the truth. "Do you have any idea what it's like to constantly be on the road?"

"As a matter of fact, I do."

"Then you know how tired you get, how tedious all the continuous travel can be. And how helpful it is to have something to help you cope."

"It's not always easy, but drugs are only going to make it harder on you and your family."

"I haven't heard my sister or my wife complain. And I know it makes me feel good," he argued.

"Feeling good and being good are two different things. That sadness you feel afterward? That's a part of the effect it has on you. Is that good? It's why you had trouble breathing too."

"And how do you know so much about what it does?" he asked.

"I know people who have been hooked on it. I tried to help a woman suffering from that dependency once, but she ended up dead. She didn't even mean to kill herself with it. She just took more and more of it to get the same short-lived happiness she felt at the first until it was just too much at once. You don't control it. It controls you."

He didn't look moved.

"And I also know about addiction on a more intimate level. I used to drink quite a bit and sometimes I still want to, I'll admit, but by the grace of God, the pull it has on you can be overcome."

"Well, I appreciate your concern, but it's too helpful for me to want to give up. I didn't find anyone here in Austin who wanted the life of an actor, so get ready. It's on to the next town or city tomorrow." And he walked off.

He was disappointed that they weren't free of the acting, but he was even more disappointed that Francis didn't even acknowledge that he had a problem for there was no way to help a person who didn't want to be helped.

"Well, we can always pray for him," Lucille said after he told her about it as they were going to sleep.

"Pray for some other actors while you're at it."

She grinned. "I already have been. From day one."

***

Lucille carried her washboard and the dirty clothes down to the river where Evelyn was carefully washing the costumes.

"It's nice to have somebody to talk with while you work, ain't it? Helps make the time pass easier."

Evelyn gave a noncommittal shrug and looked a little bit nervous.

Lucille decided it was better to break the ice. "We found out Francis takes laudanum regular." She didn't make eye contact but started with Michael's diapers first.

Evelyn didn't say anything.

"You know sometimes that causes a terrible strain on a marriage. Them spending all that money on the drug that they just have to have. And it can change a person too. Make them dangerous even. I just want you to know that I can be a pretty good listener even though it seems like I never stop talking. And you wouldn't be the first I've talked to in a similar situation either."

"He's a good man," Evelyn said fiercely.

"I didn't say he wasn't," Lucille answered gently.

She realized immediately she was being over-defensive. "I'm sorry. I just wish you'd have known him before. Breaking into the business back East wasn't as easy as I thought. There were plenty of pretty English girls who could act back in New York, and I was hungry. Going back home wasn't an option. Francis took me under his wing before he'd seen a second of my acting."

"And ya'll fell in love working together?"

"Indeed, we did."

There was a long pause as she studied the makeup that still covered the area around Evelyn's eyes. "He hits you sometimes, doesn't he?"

"Mostly the laudanum makes him calm, but when he doesn't have it or realizes he's about out, he can get a little upset. More than a little upset. He was expecting, hoping, that there would be laudanum in Austin, and there wasn't. And heaven help you if you come between him and the bottle like trying to suggest maybe he shouldn't take so much or hiding it from him. That's his first love."

"It's that way whenever someone is in the throes of addiction, but if you can get them through withdrawal, it's much easier for them to resist it."

Evelyn looked hopeful now. "You do have experience with this, don't you? You think you can help my husband?"

"I'm not a miracle worker, but Charlie and I will do everything we can to help. In the end, it won't matter if your husband won't accept any assistance. My best advice to you is to pray because God is in the business of miracles, and He can help when no one else can."

"Thank you, and I will."

"And protect yourself. It may seem hard at first, but let him know you won't stand for him hitting you again. I know there aren't many options for leaving, but there are some."

"But you're a religious woman. And you're suggesting I leave my husband?"

"I am saying is your safety is important, and no man has the right to hit you, not even your husband. You have the biblical right to physically separate from him and live separately if need be, keeping in mind that you can always return if things change."

She was such a long time in answering that Lucille didn't think she was going to, but at last, she said, "I'll remember that."

Chapter 9

Allie celebrated her fifth birthday somewhere between Austin and San Antonio.

Lucille made her a cake in the frying pan. Maybe not as good as it would have been baked and had there been more ingredients on hand, but Allie was thrilled with it and especially with the store-brought doll that had been her gift. It was a lovely doll with rosy cheeks, china blue eyes, blonde hair, and the sweetest little, brown outfit.

The Wilkersons even gave her dark, silken red ribbons for her hair, which was getting long enough to start braiding.

At the end of the day, Allie commented after prayers, "The Lord sure has blessed us, hasn't He, Momma?"

"He sure has, angel," Lucille replied, tenderly pushing her hair back.

And it wasn't but the next day that Allie asked, "Little kids can be bad, can't they, Momma?"

Lucille, who was working on darning one of Charlie's socks while the horses were getting watered, replied, "Everybody's bad sometimes, honey, even if we don't want to be. That's what the curse of sin does. Nobody's all good but the Lord."

"And sin makes God very sad. Momma, do little kids go to hell?"

She put the sock down and looked her in the eyes. "No. You have to be old enough to be able to choose whether you want to follow Jesus or go the devil's way. But God loves all His people young and old, and He gives us as many chances as He can to choose Him. The Bible tells us that He doesn't want any of us to have to go there."

"So I won't go to hell?" Allie asked, wanting to be sure.

"We don't have to be afraid of hell because Jesus took our punishment for us. And all we have to do to accept the free gift, when we're old enough to understand it, is tell Him we're sorry and ask Him into our heart and life. 'If thou shalt confess with thy mouth the Lord Jesus, and shalt believe in thine heart that God hath raised Him from the dead, thou shalt be saved.'"

"I am sorry, and I do believe that."

"That makes me very happy to hear," Lucille said, picking the sock back up.

"Can I ask God into my heart and life now?"

Lucille stopped the darning again, momentarily surprised, she said, "Well, of course you can if you really want to." She enveloped her in a hug.

"Can you pray with me?"

"Sure I can. Just say the prayer with me." She bowed her head, but then she looked back up. "You know there's no magic words, don't you? You got to mean this with all your heart."

"I know," Allie insisted in earnest.

So Lucille bowed her head and closed her eyes and so did Allie.

"I know I sin and that You sent Jesus to save me from those sins."

Her daughter repeated the words with true feeling that greatly relaxed Lucille.

"I know that He died on the cross and rose again three days later and is alive today and is coming again."

She stumbled toward the end on remembering the long string of words, but Lucille helped her.

"Lord, forgive me. Come into my life and change me."

Lucille struggled not to cry happy tears when her little girl repeated the words.

"And help me follow You all the days of my life."

Any misgivings she'd had that Allie didn't understand enough to know what she was doing or saying were completely gone.

"Thank you for saving me so that I can live in heaven someday. Amen."

Lucille pulled her into another hug as soon as she finished the amen. *And thank You for Allie,* Lucille added silently to herself. She hadn't expected that she'd come to the Lord so young, but nothing could have made her happier.

"So can I be bap-a-tized?" She'd watched enough people coming to the Lord at the revivals to know baptism followed confession.

Lucille smiled, reminded of the Ethiopian who asked what hindered him from being baptized. "I don't see why not. There's a river, isn't there? We'll just get your daddy and Michael and get ourselves on down to the river."

They told Charlie together as soon as he was done with the horses, and he was as happy over the news as Lucille was and proud too.

"Don't that beat all," he said to Allie. "I'm mighty proud of you, pumpkin. And I know God is too. Starting out following Him so young will be a big help. Believe me, I know. I wish I'd been smart enough to accept Him as a child."

Francis, who'd overheard asked, "Isn't she a little young to be baptized?"

"A little old in some churches," Evelyn pointed out. "We baptize our children as babies in the Church of England."

"It's the beauty of the gospel," Lucille answered. "Wondrous enough to confound the most brilliant minds, and yet, simple enough that even a child can understand."

They went down to the river. Francis, Evelyn, and Permelia went too.

Charlie waded out into the shallow part of the river with Allie where he explained to her that he was going to briefly dunk her in and that she had to hold her breath until she came up, but of course, Allie had seen countless baptisms in her short life and knew the drill.

"I baptize you, Allie Fiona Addington, in the name of the Father, the Son, and the Holy Ghost." He immersed her." Buried with Him in baptism." He brought her back out. "And raised to walk in the newness of life."

The Wilkersons applauded.

Lucille hugged the dripping Allie as soon as she was on dry land. As Allie had said, the Lord sure had blessed them.

***

Lucille practiced at the piano as the morning passed due to Francis sleeping in once again. Charlie had gone off to see if he could nab some game. She had Michael in her lap, and he banged on the piano once in a while, trying to add in his own music.

Allie came up to them.

"You want to play at the piano too?" Lucille asked.

She shook her head. "Not right now. Ms. Permelia's showing me how to work the puppets with the strings."

"That sounds like fun."

"I just wanted to ask you do I get to have a Bible of my very own now?" She eyed her mother's Bible that was sharing a place on the bench.

"Well, it helps, sweetheart, to be able to read it first, but we'll see. Christmas ain't too far away, and you got to show us you can be really careful with an important book."

"I will. I promise! Thank you, Momma!" She skipped off with an enthusiasm that made Lucille chuckle.

Evelyn was nearby, and she commented, "I enjoyed watching your daughter get baptized. You know something adorable? She found freedom the same day as the thirteen colonies did, July 4th." Her eyes dropped down. "I need to get back in touch with God. I'm afraid I've let things of that nature slip."

"Well, God's always waiting to hear from us, however far we've wandered, and when we spend time in His Word, you'd be amazed at how close you begin to feel to Him again. Scripture is a powerful thing because of the Author."

She paused to free her hair from Michael's death grip. He had somehow managed to get a few strands loose from her bun. "I've been thinking on your situation. What about his sister? Does she know what all's going on?"

"Permelia knows, but she prefers to ignore it."

Francis finally poked his head out of the wagon, looking worse for the wear.

Lucille gave Michael to Evelyn. "I'll talk to him now if you want me to."

Evelyn nodded, and Lucille made her way over to Francis.

"How you feeling?" she asked.

He looked surprised to be asked. "Alright, I guess."

"Are you really? You know your wife's concerned for you too."

"Is she now?" His upper lip curled and his eyes hardened, not the reaction she'd hoped it would elicit.

She was quick to remind him. "She loves you. She wants what's best for you. And that tincture is not what's best and you know it."

The target of his anger became Lucille now. "Would you just leave a man in peace?"

"I'll get out of your hair, but it's a real shame they don't make a tincture for the tincture."

***

Charlie came back with a jackrabbit, and they put in a good day of travel considering the late start. Francis rode the horses harder to make up for it.

"You been talking about our personal business to the Addingtons?" Francis demanded of Evelyn that night when he thought everyone was asleep by the campfire.

His voice was loud enough that Charlie and Lucille, who were still awake, heard.

"No, they figured everything out for themselves, but I'm glad they did. I still remember how happy our first year of marriage was before you discover the laudanum. I want it to be that way again. But mostly I want you fully well."

"No, you want me to stop buying it, so you'll have more money for you. You may be pretty and young, but that doesn't mean you can wrap me around your finger."

"You are barmy if that's what you think that's what this is about. And here's another thing, I'm not going to let you hit me anymore. I can leave with Lucille and Charlie, and I will if I have to."

"And who says I'd let you leave?" Francis asked.

"I say you'll let her leave," Charlie said, stepping into the firelight where he could be seen with his drawn gun.

Francis in stony silence walked into the wagon to sleep as cold as it was, away from them all

***

The next morning, Lucille found Permelia, who immediately asked her, "What's wrong? You look like you got something on your mind."

"I do. It's about Francis and his problem with laudanum. I've tried to get through to him. Charlie's tried. And Evelyn's tried. Maybe you can succeed where we failed. After all, you've known him longer than anybody."

"Look, my brother and me haven't had a fight since we were kids. We love each other, but we leave each other alone. He's a grown man, capable of making his own decisions. What he takes or does is not my business."

"The laudanum is your business. If you loved him, you wouldn't ignore what he's doing to his health."

She sighed. "I guess maybe I could just talk to him. Gently suggest some things."

She kept her promise, and Francis willingly went into the wagon with his sister for a private conversation, looking pleasant enough, which meant he had no idea what she was going to talk about.

He came out enraged, and he turned on Lucille and Charlie. "That talk was your doing, I know. You know I'm really starting to wish I'd left you two in the desert."

Chapter 10

Things were tense after that with Francis not speaking as much as he had before.

They came upon a small mine, and small didn't begin to describe it, as it was really only a handful of miners digging up enough for personal use and to have a little left to sell to some of the stores and blacksmiths for a slight profit.

One of the men came up to their stopped wagon; he was covered from head to toe in black coal dust.

"My daddy's black," Allie said shyly. "Sometimes."

Lucille coughed hard to hide her laughter, and Charlie flushed red.

"Oh, yeah?" the man asked, amused. "Does he like to dig too?"

She shook her head. "He paints himself black."

The man laughed. "Now that I'd like to see. You all got plans to put on a show?"

Francis spoke up. "We put on a show wherever there's interest."

"We'd love to watch your show, but we're not wealthy by any means. If we were, we'd hire somebody else to dig up this coal."

"Well, admission usually costs four cents a ticket, but we'll let you good people see it for a penny each and some coal," Francis said, showing himself to be a sharp negotiator as the coal would likely make up for the lost income.

Lucille looked at the coal closer. It was low grade coal, mostly a soft brown rather than the hard black coal she'd dug up with her cousins for fun as a child, but it burned just the same. It'd be a good heat source.

So that evening after the miners had finished their digging, they put on a show for them. They seemed to like Charlie's folk song better than the drama. They asked him to sing it again at the close of the show. He was still tuning his guitar when Allie came padding out to Lucille in her night clothes.

"You shouldn't still be up," Lucille chastised gently.

"I couldn't sleep." She climbed into her mother's waiting lap. "And I want to hear Daddy sing."

"Well, Daddy is pretty good at getting people to sleep with his singing."

Finally satisfied with the tuning, Charlie began,

"One Sunday morning, Lord, Lord, Lord
The preacher went a hunting, Lord, Lord, Lord

And he carried along a shotgun, Lord, Lord, Lord
And along came a grey goose, Lord, Lord, Lord
Well he shot down a grey goose, Lord, Lord, Lord
And the gun went a-boom-boom, Lord, Lord, Lord
And down come the grey goose, Lord, Lord, Lord
Took six weeks of falling, Lord, Lord, Lord
And six weeks calling, Lord, Lord, Lord
And they put him on the table, Lord, Lord, Lord
And your wife and my wife, Lord, Lord, Lord
There's time for feather pickin', Lord, Lord, Lord
But the fork wouldn't stick it, Lord, Lord, Lord
And the knife wouldn't cut it, Lord, Lord, Lord
And they put him in the oven, Lord, Lord, Lord
But the oven wouldn't burn him, Lord, Lord, Lord
And they him in the hog pen, Lord, Lord, Lord
But the hog couldn't eat it, Lord, Lord, Lord
And he broke the hogs teeth out, Lord, Lord, Lord
So they threw him in the sawmill, Lord, Lord, Lord
And the sawmill wouldn't cut him, Lord, Lord, Lord
And he broke the saws teeth off, Lord, Lord, Lord
And the last time I seen him, Lord, Lord, Lord
She was flyin' cross the ocean, Lord, Lord, Lord
With a long string o' goslings, Lord, Lord, Lord
And they're all goin' quack, quack, Lord, Lord, Lord."

Allie was still awake at the end of the song. "Momma,
why couldn't they eat the goose?"

It's just a silly song. It didn't really happen, but the
idea is people shouldn't go hunting on Sundays
because it's work. Least of all a preacher who should
be inside a church preaching on a Sunday morning. It
was the Lord's way of reminding him of that."

"Oh."

Charlie had come over, and he picked Allie up with one arm. "I think I got me a goose."

Allie giggled, knowing he was teasing. "No, Daddy."

"Oh, it's just a little girl then. I was confused because she wasn't in her bed."

Allie giggled again and Charlie asked Lucille, "You coming, Mother Goose, to put this gosling to bed?"

"Right behind you."

✲

They finally reached San Antonio. Big cities in the West weren't the same as big cities in the East and though this one was the once capital of the Spanish Texas, it wasn't very impressive in building or people. Most of the people looked dirt poor.

"It'll have to do," Francis said. "I guess the lack of culture comes with the territory." One of the reasons they did so well out here was that there was hardly any competition, so one couldn't expect booming, polished cities.

They weren't low on attendees when it got close to the performance. People lined up early.

Charlie and Lucille were putting Michael to bed just before the show. They were already in their first set of costumes and had just got him tucked into Charlie's empty, padded guitar case.

"I don't think Francis would ever hurt the children even as angry as he was at us for talking to him about his problem and getting his family to talk to him," Lucille said, "but still I worry. Men like that can be unpredictable. I don't know that I want to go back out into the wilderness with him."

"Me either and I kind of hope Evelyn'll decide to leave too if he refuses to get off laudanum, since we won't be there to help her. One thing's for sure, I will find that man some actors this time if I have to," Charlie said. "And besides that, I don't know how many more nights I can take of the same corny, tired lines. 'Clara, my lovely. Clara, my sweet.'"

"Clara," Michael said, sitting back up.

Neither Charlie nor Lucille said a word at first. They only stared in disbelief at their towheaded son.

Lucille spoke first. "Our baby's first word is Clara."

"Don't take it personal. Maybe he just really likes blondes," Charlie said. "He does watch Evelyn like a hawk I've noticed."

Hand still to her mouth in dismay, she nudged Charlie sharply with her elbow. "I don't find this funny. Not one little bit. Maybe it was only babble. Maybe he didn't really say it."

"Clara," Michael said again as plain as day as if to clarify it for them.

"We have got to get out of this business or who know what our kids will pick up next," she warned.

"You're being overdramatic. I think it's cute and how many kids can say their first word was Clara? Not many I'd wager. And it's not like he picked up a four letter word. Think how embarrassing that would have been."

She just rolled her eyes and bent down to kiss Michael's forehead after laying him back down. "Couldn't you have just said Mama? Is that so hard to say?"

"You could change your name to Clara," Charlie suggested.

"If I never hear that name again, it'll be too soon," she said, straightening herself again.

"Clara, Clara, Clara," her son said almost gleefully.

"Heaven have mercy," Lucille said, raising her eyes heavenward.

Chapter 11

Lucille was still in her Guildenstein costume at the end of it and was on her way to go change when she bumped into a strange man. "I'm sorry," she apologized immediately. She looked around. It should have been clear enough this space was for the actors. "You lost?"

"Not at all. You're just beautiful. Has anyone ever told you that?"

"As a matter of fact, yes. My husband," she said, putting special emphasis on the word husband. "I'm married to Othello."

He didn't seem phased by that. "I can show you a good time." He flashed some cash. "I'm sure your husband wouldn't care if we had a little fun."

"I'm sure he would, and so would I. And God cares. Not to mention my two children."

But he still didn't seem too put-off. "You saying you wouldn't want to earn some extra money? You couldn't be earning very much split between all of you."

Sometimes the only thing left to do was quote Scripture to spell it out for people. "Marriage is honourable in all, and the bed undefiled: but whoremongers and adulterers God will judge."

The man had the gall to step in closer as if to steal a kiss, but Evelyn appeared beside her, brandishing a knife. "She said no, sir. You better get out of here before her husband comes. He's the jealous type who would just as soon shoot you as look at you."

The lie about Charlie shooting him was enough to send him scurrying back to whatever rock he crawled out from. Charlie probably would have given him a good beating though.

"Thank you," Lucille said.

"There just isn't enough women out here, and they don't expect actresses to have religion. That's the problem. They think we're loose, married or not. Better to carry a weapon, so they listen when we tell them we're not."

Lucille watched her tuck the knife back into her costume. "I guess that's good advice."

***

Allie thought Michael's first word was just hilarious when she heard. Even she knew at her age that mama and dada were the norm. She proceeded to tell Permelia about it. Then she told Evelyn. She even told Francis, who she was usually reserved with.

"Maybe we haven't been spending enough time with him," Lucille worried as she bounced Michael on her knee.

"I still think you're reading too much into it," Charlie said. "It was probably just easier for him to say, and he's certainly heard it enough over the past few weeks."

"You're right," she said. Nonetheless, she was repeating and using "Mama" to him every chance she got.

That afternoon Evelyn and Permelia were getting some food together.

"You going on a picnic?" Lucille asked, looking at the heavily loaded basket.

"Not exactly," Evelyn said. "We heard there's a band of migrants and we think we saw a couple of their kids peeking at the show last evening. They looked so hungry. Practically skin and bones."

"Poor little mites," Permelia said. "I can't stand to think about them being hungry, so we're getting some food together to take to them."

"That's very kind," Lucille said.

"Well, outcasts have to help fellow outcasts, don't they?" Permelia asked with a humorous twinkle in her eye.

"I don't know about that, but I know children of God have to help children of God, and the migrants were made in His image the same as anybody else. We've got some things we can give from our supplies too. I'd love to meet them."

"We'll all go," Charlie said. He knew the people were probably harmless, but then one did hear stories of kidnapped children and the like. It always paid to be cautious.

They found that the gypsies were quite friendly and appreciative of the food. They weren't too proud to accept help. They put on a show of their own with dancing and music in payment for the food, which Allie and Michael loved.

When they got back, Francis was still out looking for actors as he had been that morning. Charlie and Lucille could tell Evelyn was a little worried about it, so they offered to go looking for him if they would watch the children, which they agreed to.

There weren't too many places he could be. Charlie saw a church and wondered if that was the very chapel where the Battle of the Alamo had taken place only a few years before. The battle where Davy Crockett had died.

There was a man he wished he'd gotten to meet. He wondered how much of the man was fact and how much of him was myth.

"I think I see him," Lucille said, pointing to the window of a store. The glass was too low-quality to tell for sure, so they went inside to see.

"I'm telling you I don't carry tincture of opium," a young storekeeper was saying to Francis. "That hasn't changed since this morning. I can order it for you. And I do have calomel."

"I don't want calomel!" Francis shouted, banging his fist on the counter. "And I can't wait around for you to order some. I need it now!"

"Look, here. You're not going to yell in my store. I'll call in a ranger to take care of you." Rangers being the local law enforcement in Texas.

Lucille spoke up. "We'll take care of him, sir. Don't worry. He's with us."

Charlie was the one who went over and got him, of course. Francis thrashed in his grip, being fighting mad, but Charlie didn't let go of his shirt. "Just settle down or I'll take you over to the jail myself."

Charlie didn't really know if they had a jail in San Antonio, but then neither did Francis, and it got him to stop struggling.

Charlie took him back to their campsite and didn't let go of him until they were there. "I thought you were supposed to be out finding actors to take our place?" he asked gruffly. "Looks like to me you only had one thing on your mind."

Francis sank onto the nearby bench without making an answer.

"I'm sure he was looking for them too," Lucille said, giving the aging actor the benefit of the doubt. "Did you find any prospects?"

Maybe it was the kindness in her voice that brought on the confession, but he mumbled like a petulant child, "I haven't been looking for replacements."

"Well, why ever not?" Lucille asked, her words mixed with a gasp.

He shrugged. "Just didn't feel like it."

Charlie was angry. "Well, you'd be advised to start feeling like it. Cause we part ways here in San Antonio. We'll keep performing for you as long as you're here, but you better have two other actors with you when you go."

***

There was another performance that evening. True to their word, Charlie and Lucille performed for Francis.

They were in the middle of the melodrama. Charlie had just kidnapped "Clara" when the real drama began.

"Leave that sweet gal alone!" yelled some liquored up audience member.

Charlie didn't know whether to continue or stop the play. He couldn't tell if the man was just really getting into the storyline or he meant what he said.

Evelyn urged him on, and he figured she knew better than he did about it, so he picked up the ropes to tie her with. The drunk whipped out his colt and shot at Charlie.

Charlie, who wore his gun at all times even in costume, drew his own gun, but there was really no need. Some other members of the audience had pounced on the man already. And fortunately, the shot had been wild thanks to his lack of sobriety. Of course, if he had been sober, he wouldn't have fired in the first place.

Lucille heard the yell and the gunfire from her barely hidden place at the piano, and she ran out from behind the curtain, fearing the worst.

"Are you okay?" Lucille asked Charlie when she came up to him, feeling him to assure herself he was still whole.

"He killed that woman. He's got to be stopped. Let go of me," the drunk yelled, trying to reason with his captors, but they were hauling him away. Hopefully to the authorities to let him sleep it off.

"I'm fine. Less enthused about acting than ever, but fine." He kissed the top of her head.

They could hear Michael crying because of the noise no doubt. Allie was probably worrying too. He started to move towards them, but Lucille said, "I'll go see to the kids. You just take it easy. The sheriff or ranger or whatever it is they call them out here might want to talk to you." Then she hurried away towards the wagon where they'd been sleeping.

The crowd was murmuring, not sure whether to go or to stay.

"In light of the shooting, we will call it a night, ladies and gentlemen," Francis addressed them, "but come back tomorrow and you can see the rest of it free of charge."

That met with everyone's approval as there was some light applause, and they began to take their leave.

"I'm so sorry," Evelyn apologized to Charlie. "We should have stopped."

"No harm done," Charlie said.

"You know," Francis said to him when the audience was all gone, "I didn't like you wearing a gun because it didn't fit any of the characters, but I'm certainly glad you wore your gun tonight."

"Not that it did me any good. I was so wrapped up in doing the acting, I would've been shot if his aim was a little better."

"I just never thought anything like that could happen," Francis said, shaking his head. "It's a crazy world we live in where a person can't tell the difference between fantasy and reality. I mean what was he thinking?"

"He wasn't. Anyone who takes anything that heightens or dulls their senses is asking for trouble."

Francis knew Charlie wasn't just talking about the man, but about him too. "I would never do anything that stupid."

"You think you would never do anything that stupid, but you can't be sure. I guarantee you that man will regret what he did when he sobers up."

"I guess there's some truth to that," he admitted, but he changed the subject. "I don't get why you and your wife are so eager to leave, barring tonight obviously. You can see we get good numbers. You wouldn't go hungry. You both have a talent musically and for acting as well. This is a perfect setup. What if I offer you a salary too?"

"It's not about the money," Charlie explained. "Acting's not our calling. Our calling is to share God with the masses, to help the sick."

"As long as we're being honest, I'll tell you something else, I don't know what you people get out of God."

Lucille reappeared, holding Michael against her shoulder and walking with him to try and get him back to sleep. "And that's more troubling than your problem with laudanum," she said.

"It troubles me too," Evelyn said in a small voice.

Francis spun around and raised his hand to make a point, but she flinched because she thought he was about to hit her.

For the first time, it looked like he felt sorry for it.

"Your wife fears you," Charlie said. "Doesn't that bother you?"

He hung his head.

"You know what bothers me?" Evelyn asked. "We're having a baby, and I don't know if I can trust you around him."

Francis looked ecstatic at this unexpected news.

Permelia was thrilled too. "A little one to keep. I'm so happy."

Evelyn only continued to look somberly at her husband, which made him come back down to earth. "I will stop taking the tincture if you'll stay with me. I will never hurt you or the baby. It's a promise." He looked at Permelia. "If I do, I give you permission to see they get to safety."

He left and came back with the little that remained in the bottle of laudanum. He poured it out, making a wet, sticky spot in the earth.

"I love you," Evelyn said. "And thank you."

He stepped closer and hugged his wife. He really seemed to have meant everything he said. Whether the new baby would remain motivation enough for him to stay off the laudanum indefinitely remained to be seen.

Chapter 12

It hadn't even been a full twenty-four hours but already Francis was in the throes of withdrawal.

He hadn't slept good the previous night without his usual dose of laudanum, and he couldn't stop yawning. Beads of sweat clung to his skin. He nervously paced up and down and around the small wagon like he was looking for something.

They all took turns staying with, keeping his mind off the laudanum by reading to him or talking with him and trying to get him to get some sleep before the evening performance.

"I feel like I'm wrestling with influenza," Francis complained to Lucille when it was her shift.

"I know it seems really bad now, but it'll pass, I promise," she told him. "Can I pray with you? He will be your source of strength if you let Him."

Francis looked as if he thought the suggestion was half-baked, but it must have showed how bad he was feeling that he accepted the offer seconds later. "If you think it'll help."

"Oh, Lord, we put Francis into Your hands. Drive this temptation far from him. Turn his weakness into strength. Let this trial point him to You. Help him trust in your goodness and faithfulness. And may it all be used for Your glory. All this I pray in the name of Jesus Christ. Amen."

"You pray beautifully," Francis complimented. "But I suppose missionaries always do."

"Prayers don't have to be beautiful. It's just talking to God, laying your heart before Him."

"You know this may sound completely insane, but do you think it wasn't an accident that we stumbled onto your wagon? 'There is special providence in the fall of a sparrow' and all that," he said, quoting a line from Hamlet.

"I don't just think it. I know it. 'Man's goings are of the Lord'." She returned his Shakespeare with Scripture.

"I almost believe it. I don't remember if I told you, but my parents were theatre people too. We never had much time or use for God, but now I wish they'd raised me and Permelia with religion."

"It's definitely nice when you grow up with Him. You know my momma tells me one of my first words was Jesus. Of course, she also tells me I came out talking up a storm, so I don't know," she said with a laugh. "But it's not a requirement to be raised knowing."

"I'm a little old to know Him now," Francis said.

"As long as there's breath in your body, there's time to know God. I even think it's easier when you come to God as an adult in some ways because a child believes because they're told by their parents to believe and sometimes that makes it so they never really come to know God personally. They get wrapped up in the attending church part and think that makes them saved.

"An adult who comes to Christ later knows what they were before and what they are now by the grace of

God, and they can better understand things. But then again, it really boils down to just one question: have you opened your heart to the truth? To Jesus? Any person at any age can do that."

He grunted what sounded like agreement or at least partial agreement.

Lucille spent the rest of the time reading to him from the Bible. He finally fell asleep lulled by the psalms.

Evelyn was to relieve Lucille, and they met just outside the wagon. "How is he?" she asked.

"Finally sleeping."

"I won't disturb him then." She looked at the wagon for a few moments as if she could see through its walls and then said, "He's not having an easy time. I just don't understand why anyone would want to put themselves through this. To abuse laudanum until it comes to this."

"I don't think anyone means for it to come to this, but I believe the root of the abuse lies in man's attempt to provide something, to feel something that only God can give."

"I never thought of it that way." She sighed. "I worry he'll get back on it as soon as we're in a town that carries it."

"Praise God that he'll be fully through the hard symptoms before he's able to find it again though. That'll help a great deal."

When it was time for supper, Evelyn went in to tell him, but he wasn't in his bed.

She came back out to where everyone was holding supper. "Did any of you see Francis leave?"

No one had.

"I should've stayed by his bedside. I hope he hasn't gone out to look for laudanum," Evelyn said, biting her lip nervously.

"Where would he find any?" Charlie asked. "I think he proved to himself pretty positively yesterday that there was none to be had."

"Well, once when he was completely out, he broke into people's houses looking for some. Didn't find any, but that didn't stop him."

"Well, that wouldn't be good. The last thing he needs is trouble with the law or worse for someone to shoot him for trespassing." Lucille looked to her husband. "Maybe you should go look for him."

"Maybe I'd better," Charlie agreed. Just as he had set his bowl of stew down to get cold while he was away, Francis strolled into view with two young people. He wore an expression that said he was pleased with himself.

"Meet Ada and Moses," he said. "The replacements. Ada here is an accomplished pianist, and this boy here could act circles around John Buckstone." Moses and Ada looked as excited as Francis.

Lucille wasn't sure who John Buckstone was, but he must have been good. "Why that's wonderful."

"That's just fine. Real fine," Charlie said. "Everything seems to be coming together for you, Francis, if you don't mess up." It was more than a casual comment. It was a warning, and he hoped Francis heeded it.

***

"It's nice to see Francis treating Evelyn so good," Lucille said to Charlie as they observed him helping her up the stairs into the wagon a couple days later.

"It sure is."

"They're so different in ages. I almost wonder if he didn't feel the need to feel more rested to keep up with her, and that's why he started taking it," she speculated.

"If he wanted to feel younger, he should have married a woman older than himself."

He was teasing her because she was two year older than him. She looked over her shoulder where he was standing just behind her. "That worked out well for you, has it?"

He grinned and put his arms around her. "Extremely. A wiser, more experienced woman is the way to go. And it makes a lot more sense too when I call you my old lady."

"If you're trying to romance me, Mr. Addington, you should find some better lines than that."

He whispered something amorous into her ear, which was strongly worded enough that it made her color prettily.

She cleared her throat. "That's definitely better."

***

Lucille and Charlie had their last performance that evening. The Wilkersons did something they'd never done before it. They prayed.

"Well, I think we've won another soul to the Lord and now Permelia seems interested because of her brother," Charlie commented as they walked away from the prayer circle.

"I think Francis wants to raise his child knowing God, and to do that, he has to know Him himself."

"A child can inspire you to make a lot of changes, and God can make you a new man entirely. Francis has a real chance of making it off the laudanum."

They hardly had to think about their parts, so familiar had they become with them. They took their bows and curtseys at the end, ending their career as actors. They were glad to pass the baton to Ada and Moses, who'd been spending the past couple of days learning the lines.

"You know I think I'll kind of miss it in a way," Lucille said to Charlie as they were preparing to change out of the costumes. "Maybe we should add a drama to the revival. I think it could prove to be quite the draw."

"You have got to be joking," he said, stopping the scrubbing off of his makeup in the washbowl to look at her.

The grin proved she was, and he was quite relieved.

They worked on moving their things into a brand new wagon after they'd changed. Charlie had purchased the new wagon, which didn't look any different from the old one, just that afternoon.

It was a major disappointment to Allie, who stood staring at it for the first time. "Aw, it's not red, and it doesn't have a real roof," she said.

"We could have a flashy wagon to draw people's attention, but then we want it to be the Lord that draws people's attention, don't we?" Lucille asked her daughter.

"I reckon," Allie mumbled though it was clear she didn't really understand.

"And tomorrow we get to set out to see somewhere new," Charlie said. "Just me, you, your momma, and Michael."

Allie had missed it just being the four of them, and she loved seeing new places. "Where, Daddy?"

"Wherever the wind takes us," he said, lifting her up.

"Wherever the Lord takes us," Lucille corrected.

"And who controls the wind, pray tell?" he asked with a grin. "But if a certain little girl isn't in bed like she's supposed to be, she'll miss all the excitement of getting to try out our new wagon in the morning."

Allie jumped down from her father's arms and scurried back towards her bed, making both her parents laugh.

Lucille hadn't been totally kidding about missing the acting. It was fun to pretend to be somebody else for a little while, but she wouldn't trade her real life or her real calling for all the applause in the world.

The End

"You have got to be joking," he said, stopping the scrubbing off of his makeup in the washbowl to look at her.

The grin proved she was, and he was quite relieved.

They worked on moving their things into a brand new wagon after they'd changed. Charlie had purchased the new wagon, which didn't look any different from the old one, just that afternoon.

It was a major disappointment to Allie, who stood staring at it for the first time. "Aw, it's not red, and it doesn't have a real roof," she said.

"We could have a flashy wagon to draw people's attention, but then we want it to be the Lord that draws people's attention, don't we?" Lucille asked her daughter.

"I reckon," Allie mumbled though it was clear she didn't really understand.

"And tomorrow we get to set out to see somewhere new," Charlie said. "Just me, you, your momma, and Michael."

Allie had missed it just being the four of them, and she loved seeing new places. "Where, Daddy?"

"Wherever the wind takes us," he said, lifting her up.

"Wherever the Lord takes us," Lucille corrected.

"And who controls the wind, pray tell?" he asked with a grin. "But if a certain little girl isn't in bed like she's supposed to be, she'll miss all the excitement of getting to try out our new wagon in the morning."

Allie jumped down from her father's arms and scurried back towards her bed, making both her parents laugh.

Lucille hadn't been totally kidding about missing the acting. It was fun to pretend to be somebody else for a little while, but she wouldn't trade her real life or her real calling for all the applause in the world.

The End